Watch of Wondering Love

D.L. Wilson

To Christmas!

Acknowledgments

Thanks to Laura Gray Lewis for editing this book and helping make what comes out of my head understandable.

And thanks to Phil Salter for the lovely cover concept and art.

CONTENTS

Chapter 1

"Okay, God, here's the deal," Mary said quietly as she drove past the series of once-new strip malls. She was heading toward the canyon, watching the road, the fuel gauge, and the baby in the back seat all at the same time. "If I pass the last gas station before the fuel warning light comes on, it's your job, God, to get me through the canyon and into town." As she neared it, the last gas station looked particularly inviting and convenient, but she knew that stopping for gas (and maybe a diet cola) would wake the baby, which would mean he had to be fed, which would take at least 20 minutes, which would make her late to her sister's mother- and father-in-law's house, and subsequently late to her interview.

She slowed a little as she passed the gas station, looking at the fuel gauge needle as if it were a compass that would direct her. It was already below the E, but the light still wasn't on, so she turned her attention once again to the road ahead and drove on. Five hundred yards into the canyon, the light went on. She knew from a couple of inconvenient previous experiences that she had about 40 miles before she ran completely out of gas, and she knew that North Pine was still about 35 miles away. She considered going back for a moment, but then said, "It's all yours, God," and accelerated up the hill.

Going over her résumé and her "strength statements" in her mind, she drove quickly, but didn't speed, knowing the reputation of the local sheriff's deputies for excellent speed traps and long delays. She barely squeezed in front of an 18-wheeler as a passing lane closed. Getting behind that big fella would have sunk it all. This canyon was gorgeous in the autumn, but by this time of year the only leaves left on the trees were the curmudgeonly, wrinkly brown ones that just refused to let go and follow their comrades to the ground. Most of the trees were bare, and there was snow stretching down some of the north-facing slopes from a storm the previous week.

As she pulled out of the canyon 30 minutes later into the broad mountain valley, the baby boy began to stir. "No, no, no, no!" Mary panicked to herself. She began humming just loud enough for him to hear in his sleep, but not loud enough to wake him, "Away in a manger, no crib for his bed." It was the first lullaby that came to mind this time of year. He settled back down and his face relaxed again to the perfect chubby-cherub face she loved to see.

When she pulled into the driveway, her sister's mother-in-law stepped out, with a shawl ineffectively wrapped over one shoulder. Mary had been to this house only once before, when her sister Holly had married Andy and they held an open house in North Pine. Holly's directions were perfect, leading Mary to the house without delay.

"We thought you might not make it," Mrs. Taylor said as she took the diaper bag from Mary who was unbuckling the baby boy and trying to shield him from the cold wind.

"I might not if I don't leave immediately," Mary replied. Then, thinking that sounded abrupt she added, "I'm very grateful to you for taking Ty. I don't know what I would have done without you, Mrs. Taylor."

"Oh, call me Sharon. Your sister does." Mary could tell that Sharon wanted her daughter-in-law to call her 'Mom.' "Besides, we don't get to see babies enough at this old house. Our son and your sister don't bring little Alex and Stephanie up here nearly enough to satisfy our longing for the sound of children."

"Well, thanks all the same," replied Mary, now inside the house unloading some of the contents from the bag. "He's going to want this formula right away, and you can follow it up with some rice cereal if he still seems hungry. I should be back within an hour, so hopefully he won't need a diaper change or be too much trouble." She said this putting her hand on the doorknob, pausing to see if Sharon had any questions or further chit-chat.

"You go now," replied Sharon. "You don't want to be late for your big interview. Good luck!" she waved as Mary thanked her one last time and closed the door behind her. She might have sprinted to the car if the wind hadn't been so cold as to hint at ice, and if she hadn't been wearing a skirt.

She pulled into the parking lot three minutes before her scheduled interview. Checking herself in the mirror and finding too much out of place to address in only 30 seconds, she pulled her hair behind her ears and made sure there was no lipstick leaking out the corners of her mouth, then she grabbed the neat manila folder she had brought and rushed into the small building in front of the larger factory. The woman behind the desk looked as if she had been there since the beginning, as if the building had been built around her. It was immediately apparent that it was her office, although Mary couldn't specify why she knew this.

"Mary Comardy?"

"Yes, I'm here to see Mr. . . . ." Mary shuffled through the papers in her manila folder.

"Mr. Carter. I know. You're cutting it a little close, don't you think?" the woman said somewhere between a sneer and a motherly chiding.

"Yes, I know I'm almost . . . I'm not as early as I should be," Mary replied. "Traffic in the canyon was a little slow."

"Well, you're in luck. Mr. Carter is late returning from lunch. Please sit there and wait. It shouldn't be more than ten or twenty minutes."

Turning to the puffy leather couch the receptionist had indicated, Mary was angry and jubilant at the same time; angry because she had rushed so frantically to get there, but happy that she had time to collect her thoughts and say a desperate prayer before the interview.

By the time the receptionist led her to Mr. Carter's office, Mary was beginning to worry about Ty and Sharon. If this interview took more than 30 minutes, Sharon might have a real train wreck on her hands.

Mr. Carter welcomed Mary into his office with a handshake and an apology for his tardiness. He looked uncomfortable in his tie and short-sleeved shirt. He was a stocky man whose thick neck seemed to be constantly testing the collar for weaknesses through which to break loose. His head was completely shaven, so close that she couldn't tell if he shaved it because he was going bald or because he just liked it that way.

"Tell me a little about yourself," Mr. Carter said, apparently to the résumé he was staring at.

She had practiced this piece two dozen times in the mirror. "I'm a quick learner with a passion for doing things right. In my last job at the Rockwell plant down in Sunset, I worked my way up in only nine months from an assembly worker to a functional cell captain, where I helped to bring down the defects rate in my cell by 40%. I'm easy to get along with, and I work hard—and smart."

"I don't see any college or trade school on your résumé."

"No sir. I've been wanting to go to college, but life's been getting in the way," she said with an easy grin. She had practiced all these lines.

"Well, part of the reason Rockwell went out of business is that it didn't keep up with technology," Mr. Carter replied, still looking at the résumé. "It kept paying people to do what computers can do—and do better—and that's why it got shut out of the market by the Mexicans and the Chinese. I've kept Black Star in business with current technology, which requires some pretty serious math and computer skills. I don't see that kind of stuff on your résumé."

"You're right sir, it's not there; but I'm smart. I passed the AP Calculus test in high school, and I've been working with my brother-in-law to get up to date with some of the software that's out there. I may not meet all the criteria in the job description, but I'm not afraid of any of it."

He glanced up at her. "That's what people say who don't have enough experience but still want the job."

This knocked her off balance. Up until now, the classes she had taken at the employment service, the YouTube videos she had watched, and the hours of practice she had done with her sister were paying off beautifully. But with his last statement, he had moved all the playing pieces of the game. She felt her neck and ears start to warm. "When you're nervous, be honest," she heard one of her employment service job coaches say in her head. "If you try to get cute when you're nervous, you'll blow up."

"You're right Mr. Carter. I don't have all the experience listed in the job description, but I do still want it. I know if you give me a chance, I can do it."

"We don't have the time or money for much on-the-job training. I just don't think I can put you into the position you applied for."

"Give me a chance to prove myself. You'll be so glad you did."

Mr. Carter sat back in his chair and looked at her. "I'll tell you what. Although I can't put you in the position you applied for, there's another that I think you can fill. It's more manual, and for less money, but I'll keep an eye on you and see if you catch on as well as you say you can. And if you do, we love to hire from within."

Mary was excited, but she replied, "How much less would the pay be? I don't know if I would still be able to accept it."

"A dollar less per hour. Would you still want it?"

Calculating in her head, Mary held the $160 difference up against her monthly budget she had memorized. It would be tight but workable if she whittled in a couple more places or made a little extra money on the side or by picking up overtime. "What is the job? I have to know if I would like it and if it's within what I want for my career path."

"It's a quality assurance position. You would be checking finished goods for accuracy. We do work here the Chinese and Mexicans can't duplicate because we have to have our product perfect to within a sixteenth of the width of a human hair." Mr. Carter shook his head at her confused look. "You won't really be measuring the pieces. We have lasers do that. You'll just be moving pieces around, loading them into the measuring instruments, stuff like that."

"That sounds okay," replied Mary, getting back onto comfortable, rehearsed ground. "Would there be opportunities for personal development and growth within the company?"

"You mean do we reimburse college tuition and can you get promoted? Yes, after a year, and yes, if you prove yourself competent."

Again, Mr. Carter's candor destabilized Mary's script. "Oh. Okay," she replied.

"Well?" he asked, "is the position within your 'career aspirations'?"

"Yes," responded Mary as confidently as she could muster. "When do I start?"

"The Monday after Thanksgiving," Mr. Carter said standing with her résumé in his hand. "We can't afford to pay you for two holidays just for coming in, taking a tour, and filling out a W-4."

"Right," she responded, standing also. "Thanks for giving me the chance. I'll be the best thing you've seen around here in ages," she said shaking Mr. Carter's hand.

He walked her to the front desk and handed her résumé to the receptionist. "Betty, Ms. Comardy will be joining the QA team on the Monday after Thanksgiving. Can you get everything ready for that to happen?"

"Sure," replied Betty who, after Mr. Carter had said his good-byes and walked away, cocked her head to the side and looked Mary up and down.

In the awkward silence, Mary stuck out her hand. "Thanks for your help, Betty. I look forward to working with you."

Betty waved as she took the résumé and swiveled around to a large filing cabinet.

Mary hesitantly turned toward the door, looking back twice. But remembering Ty and his probable state, she hustled into the parking lot, giving thanks early for the chance she'd just been given.

Chapter 2

"Gas station or Sharon's?" she asked herself. Muttering a halting prayer, she drove in the direction of Sharon's home. Her car died 150 yards short of a gas station. She texted her sister Holly for Sharon's number. When nothing came back immediately, she stepped out of the car and began to push against the inside frame of the door, rocking it forward, but not building any rolling momentum. Her skirt and heels made the job harder—and colder. A pickup truck pulled up behind her, and two boys who looked to be in their late teens climbed out. They didn't bother to ask if they could help; they just threw their weight into the back of the car.

"Jump in and steer," one grunted. "You just going to the gas station . . . I hope?" he asked through heavy breaths.

"Yes," she called back. The car began to roll faster. By the time she pulled off the road into the gas station, the boys were trotting alongside the car with only one hand on it, as though guiding it. As she pulled up to the pump, she looked in her rearview mirror and saw that they had already turned back toward their truck.

"Boys, can I buy you a soda, or hot cocoa or something to thank you for your help?"

They looked at each other, one shrugged, and they walked back to her car as she started the pump flowing.

Inside the warm gas station, the boys each picked out a soda while Mary got a hot cocoa. "I prefer my poison to be hot at this time of year," she said, striving to make conversation. The boys smiled politely.

As they walked back out into the cold, Mary said again, "Thanks for stopping. You two are my heroes today."

"Well, we usually try to help a lady who needs it," said one.

The other smiled, "And we didn't see the baby seat until it was too late."

The first boy shook his head and turned toward the truck. "Thanks, ma'am," he said, raising his soda.

Mary dismissed the "ma'am" in her mind and smiled. "So far," she thought, "I like 80% of the people I've met in this town."

***

She shuffled as fast as her heels would let her up the walk to Sharon's house. It had probably been built in the 50's, sitting white, squat and small, but looking comfortable on its ample lot, surrounded by a three-foot chain-link fence. It had been there long enough for some slow-growing trees to become overgrown. Mary expected to hear Ty's screams before the door was opened, but instead, when Sharon's husband Bill answered Mary's soft knock, she saw Ty sleeping on Sharon's shoulder.

"So soon?" Sharon lamented softly as Mary walked over to her boy.

"Did he give you too much trouble?" Mary asked quietly. She wanted to take her son, but she didn't want to wake him, so she awkwardly folded her arms.

"He was an angel once we changed his diaper and got some food in him," responded Sharon. "I bet you're hungry, too," she said to Mary, who suddenly registered the wonderful smell of the house and instantly felt famished. She looked at her watch. It was past 2:30, Ty's naptime.

"What time did he fall asleep?" she asked.

"Just a few minutes ago. Look, let's put him down in the crib and feed you," said Sharon, standing up carefully with the boy against her shoulder. "Yes, we have a crib," she responded to Mary's quizzical look. "We keep one set up in case your sister and her recluse husband ever bring our grandbabies up to visit us."

Mary knew that Holly visited once in a while, and that it wasn't as frequently as Sharon and Bill would like.

Sharon laid the boy down in the crib in a room down the hall and closed the door. She listened for a second at the door, and then whispered, "All clear."

"How'd your interview go?" asked Sharon, collecting a bowl and a spoon. "Is chicken noodle soup alright?"

Mary laughed inside, thinking, "Of course it's chicken noodle soup! What else would this perfect little grandma serve? And it's homemade!" she thought gleefully as Sharon put the steaming bowl in front of her, complete with a cloth napkin.

"This smells divine," Mary said as she blew on the soup, stirred it a bit and took a careful bite. She inhaled sharply to cool the delicious broth.

"When do you find out if you got the job?" Sharon asked sitting beside her and fiddling with another napkin.

"Well, I kind of already did. I didn't get the one I applied for, but I got a different one. He offered it to me right on the spot."

"That's great! When do you start?"

"The Monday after Thanksgiving. Which kind of puts me in a bind," Mary said, relaxing more with each bite of soup. "I expected to first, feel how the interview went, then start to look for an apartment if it went well and I got maybe a second interview. Now I have to find an apartment and move in just a week and a half."

"Well, why don't you stay here while you're looking?" Sharon offered.

Bill cleared his throat in the front room.

"Oh, you hush, Bill! This sweet girl and her sweet baby boy need a place for a few weeks. And heaven knows we've got room." Mary had forgotten that Bill was even in the house. Then Sharon said to Mary, "How he can hear that and miss most every other word I say . . . ."

"Oh, I wouldn't want to impose on you," Mary replied. "You've both been so kind just today. I couldn't ask more from you."

"You're not asking anything of us. We're asking of you: will you please do us the honor of bringing that little ray of sunshine into our home, even if it's only for a couple of weeks? Will you please allow us to help you? Bill is half-retired—heaven help me—and we have too much time on our hands as it is. We want to do a church mission to some faraway land, but we're not quite ready for that yet. So we need something to keep us out of trouble."

Mary was pragmatic. She understood that travelling from Sunset to North Pine even a couple of times to look for a place to live would cost a fortune in gas and babysitting (unless Holly could watch Ty, in which case she would have to pay in other ways). Living with Grandma and Grandpa Taylor would allow her to take her time to find the right place without the stress of commuting and finding sitters while trying to start a new job. Besides, she liked Sharon.

"Well, if you insist," Mary said in the same playful tone Sharon had been using to convince her.

"Oh, I do. I certainly do."

The volume on Bill's game increased, and Sharon and Mary smiled conspiratorially.

Chapter 3

"Why on earth would you want to do that?" asked Holly over the phone.

"Are you kidding me? This is a huge blessing for me. Sharon is the sweetest little grandma," Mary said into her cell phone as she exited the freeway into Sunset.

"Sharon? She sure seems that way, doesn't she? But just wait until you move in. She'll be judging you so hard, you'll feel like you're naked on *The People's Court*."

"I don't see it in her."

"Well, you didn't ruin her perfect little 'Andrew's' life by marrying him and giving him two babies. So maybe she'll go a little easier on you than she does on me. I'm telling you, I can't stand to visit her. I know she wants us to go up there more, but I can't bring myself to do it. And Andy supports me in that."

"Andy gives into you in that," replied Mary.

"I don't control that man. If he wanted to go to his mommy's house every weekend, I'd go with him—and try to act civil."

"Do you wonder why he. . . ." Mary gave up. "Well, it should only be for a couple of weeks while I find another place for Ty and me."

"You better hope so. I'm dreading going up there for Thanksgiving."

"You're going there for Thanksgiving? I thought we were taking mom to Uncle Steve's."

"No, Andy says we've gone to Thanksgiving with my side of the family three of the last four years, so it's time we went up to his parents'. Besides, his brothers will be there, and I get along with their wives, so it won't be so bad."

"Hey, crazy thought," Mary said. "Could I come to Thanksgiving with you at the Taylors'? You could help me move my stuff up that day and then I could just stay there. Please," she pleaded at Holly's delay. "I could really use a couple of extra sets of hands. Heaven knows I don't have much to move, but it's a lot for just me."

"Fine. Should we invite mom, too?" Holly responded sarcastically, as if mom were an entire platoon.

"Sure, unless Uncle Steve wants to pick her up or she wants to drive down there. You know how she hates to drive long distances, though."

Holly exhaled audibly on the other end of the line. "I can't make that decision. I'll have to talk to Andy. It's his family, and I can't impose you and mom on them."

"Great!" replied Mary, knowing that Andy would be very willing to help and host her. He was the kind of man who drove in the right lane just in case there was a stranded car. He picked up hitch-hikers and loaned out power tools. On the way back to the Taylors' from Holly and Andy's open house years before, Andy and Bill had stopped the cars to try to free a deer that had gotten its hoof twisted and trapped in a barbed-wire fence. The doe had been struggling long enough that the wire had peeled back and gathered up the skin from a six-inch length of her foreleg, and she was in no mood to patiently await Andy and Bill's heroism. Andy came away from the experience with a big grin, several deep bruises, and what he called "an appreciative nuzzle," a bite the size of a small apple just outside his shin bone.

"Well, I'm home," Mary said to Holly as she pulled into their mother's driveway. "I'll talk to you later. Thanks for helping me out."

"It's not for sure. I'll talk to Andy. Talk to you later. Give mom a kiss for me," Holly said and hung up.

Mary climbed out, slung the diaper bag over her shoulder, and got Ty out of his car seat.

"So glad you're home," her mom half-whispered, glancing up from her show. Ty's head popped off Mary's shoulder as if he thought he might miss something, but his eyes were still unstable in their sockets, rolling around a little. "Hi sunshine," the grandma said to Ty, then again to Mary, "How'd the interview go?"

Chapter 4

Mary and Mark got married six months after meeting in the break room at Rockwell.

Mark was rocking and dropping the vending machine as quietly as one can drop a vending machine. But the snack bag clung to the metal coil. Mary walked up behind him, not intending to sneak. But seeing that he didn't notice her, she got a little closer before clearing her throat. Mark spun around so quickly that Mary stumbled backward. Mark caught her wrist, and instantly began apologizing. "I'm sorry, I didn't know who it was, I didn't know it was you, my Gardetto's won't fall, and I'm just trying to get a snack, those vending guys can get pretty bent out of shape if they see you roughing up their machines. . . ."

Once Mary got her feet firmly under her, she smiled and without a word went to the vending machine, inserted a dollar, and punched in the code for Gardetto's. Two bags fell, and she swept them both out of the machine.

"Thanks." said Mark, reaching out his hand. Mary simply raised her eyebrows.

"I paid for one of those packages," Mark said, feeling awkward about keeping his hand extended.

"And yet, Karma gave them both to me," replied Mary. "Tell you what: I'll sell it to you. Fifty cents."

"I just paid seventy-five cents for it. I'm not going to pay a dollar twenty-five for a bag of Gardetto's."

"Don't think of it as paying a dollar twenty-five. Think of it as losing seventy-five cents, and then finding a friend who would give you a new bag for thirty-three percent off."

"Forget it," Mark said, not wanting to give her the satisfaction. He turned and walked away when a bag of Gardetto's hit the back of his shoulder and fell to the ground.

"Cmon, we're just having fun, right?" Mary teased.

"It appears that one of us is," Mark responded, picking up the bag and continuing to walk toward the door of the break room.

"Hang on, I'm sorry," Mary said. "Don't be mad. You don't even know my name; how can you curse me if you don't know my name?"

Mark rolled his eyes and shook his head slightly, turning his attention to opening his Gardetto's.

"It's Mary."

"Okay, I guess now I can curse you," Mark said, walking out the door.

"But you won't, right?" Mary called through the closing door.

The next Monday, Mark jogged up behind Mary as they walked through the huge parking lot toward the factory entrance.

"My name's Mark," he said. "I didn't think it was fair that I've been cursing your name all weekend when you can't retaliate."

"I think that's fair," Mary smiled. "But not knowing your name wasn't stopping me. If anything bad happens to you in the near future, it was probably my fault. But the more I talk to you, the more I think maybe you're not such a bad guy. So if my curses work, I'm sorry."

"Apology accepted," he said as they entered the building amid the crowd of other workers and then split up to go to their separate areas.

She didn't see him for a week, but packages of Gardetto's appeared three times at her work station that week. One of her co-workers thought it was a little creepy and asked if they shouldn't report it to management.

"And stop the supply of free Gardetto's?" joked Mary.

Mark asked her out that weekend.

***

Mary took the job at Rockwell only to make money for college. Her thinking was, "One year at Rockwell with some frugal living, and I'll have my first two years of tuition paid."

She was a smart girl coming out of high school, in the top quintile of her class. She could have ranked higher if she hadn't needed to work 25 hours a week to help with the family budget. Her father had left the family when she was in elementary school. He sent an occasional Christmas or birthday card from somewhere outside St. Louis. The only good things he left were a dogged stubbornness and enough equity in their small 1950s bungalow to keep them afloat on home refinances to occasionally supplement her mom's cashier jobs. Statisticians would have called them "working poor" until Holly and Mary were old enough to start contributing. By that time, they owed more on the house than her parents had originally bought it for, but it was home and they had a dream to keep it.

Mary's mother, Claire, insisted that she go to college. "You're too smart to waste those brains doing the jobs I've done. God gave you a good mind; you have to use it," she said, arguing against Mary's working at Rockwell.

"Mom, a one-year delay to do it right will outweigh a one-year head start and getting farther into debt."

Knowing Mary was right didn't comfort Claire or assuage her perception of how unfair it was that such a smart and good kid didn't have the advantages that so many of those snot-nosed college kids had.

Mary was six months into her one-year plan, flying high on a promotion to assistant cell captain when she met Mark. He was quirky cute, with a crooked smile and hair that wouldn't sit right. After two months of dating, Mark decided she was the one. "And since I know that," he explained during a break at work, "there's no sense putting it off. How soon do you think we can get married?"

"Don't you think you should ask me first?" inquired Mary. She said it in a kidding voice, but she really was, despite her practicality, irritated at the fact that, first, he hadn't asked her, second, he had assumed she would say yes, and third, he hadn't done something romantic.

"You're right," he responded and kissed her on the cheek as he got up at the sound of the whistle calling them back to work. "You're right," he said again as he walked away.

That Saturday night he drove her out to Chestnut Park where there was a picnic table set with a linen tablecloth, candles, and the best take-out in town. He got down on one knee and presented her with his grandmother's wedding ring. "Miss Mary Saunders, would you do me the honor of being my wife forever?"

"Good enough," she thought as she said, "Of course, yes!" and kissed him.

"Now this ring's only a place-holder," he said as he put it on her finger. "If you don't like it, we can get another. I have some money set aside for one."

"I'll have to think about it," she thought as she said, "I really like it!" It was a size and a half too big, so she had to keep her finger bent the rest of the night to keep it from slipping off.

The next week they went to the jeweler and looked for other rings, but nothing called to her more than his grandmother's, so they got it resized and she started to love it.

Three months after the wedding, one evening when he finished showering after work, he reached too far outside the tub for his towel and slipped. She heard the crash and rushed into the bathroom to find him convulsing on the floor, wrapped partially in the torn-down shower curtain, lying next to a broken-off chunk of the sink. After several surgeries, a lot of waiting and a thousand prayers, Mary had to decide whether to take him off life support. Most of his family still held out hope despite the doctors saying there was virtually none. But his family hadn't had the discussion she did with him late one night after one of those movies that made them talk about such things.

"If I'm ever in that situation, just pull the plug," he said. "I don't want to lie around piling up medical bills and wasting away. I don't want to be alive if I can't live." He was serious, so she complied. His family never spoke to her again, even at the funeral. And she didn't tell them that she was pregnant.

***

Mark's small corporate life insurance policy covered his funeral expenses and his medical bills and left just enough for Mary to buy a small new car, another promise Mark had her make on that night of the serious discussion. She tried to continue living on her own in the apartment she had shared with Mark, but found the loneliness too heavy, and so she moved back in with her mom. A couple of months later, Rockwell closed its doors, giving a meager severance package to all the employees based on rank and longevity, meaning Mary didn't get much. She looked for work, but, now showing noticeably at seven months pregnant, she was a walking health insurance bomb, so no company considered her.

And then Ty was born. The Lamaze instructor said that a mother's water rarely breaks; Mary's water broke. The Lamaze instructor said that first babies always take forever; Ty was born within an hour of Mary reaching the hospital, which meant she didn't have time for an epidural. The nurse laid the boy on Mary's chest, his puffy cheek against her skin, and Mary fell in love again, this time with little Mr. Tyson Mark Comardy.

Chapter 5

At 8:00 in the morning on Thanksgiving Day, Andy and Holly arrived to Claire's house to put all of Mary's possessions into a borrowed trailer. It only took 45 minutes (with the help of a couple of neighbors who had been bribed with cookies). Just as they were finishing loading, Uncle Steve pulled up to pick up Claire and drive her the hour and a quarter to his house.

"Looks like I showed up just in time," he called from his car as they closed the ramp to the trailer, just like a good corny uncle should say. He turned off his car and walked onto the browning lawn, his hands in his jacket pockets.

"Yes you did, just in time to give me a hug," said Mary, embracing him. "I'm moving up to North Pine, so you'll see even less of me. Thanks for coming to get Mom."

"No problem. Your Aunt Emma shooed me out of the kitchen days ago, and the football games don't start for a couple of hours, so I was glad to have something to do. I guess we're bringing her back Sunday? It sounds like the girls are going to party this weekend. That's okay though. Usually with this day-after-Thanksgiving shopping I refuse to go but Aunt Emma wakes me up at three in the morning anyway, crashing around the room to get ready, and the guilt keeps me up 'til sunrise. So this way, I don't have to feel guilty; I can sleep in 'til my prostate wakes me up at six."

Holly rolled her eyes at Uncle Steve's overplayed jokes, but Mary loved that part of him. It made him seem so predictable and stable. Uncle Steve collected Claire and her pots filled with luck for the day's impending feast.

"Mom, you've got a key to get back in the house, right? You did lock all the doors, right?" Mary reassured herself.

"Of course I did, and of course I have a key."

Mary and Claire hugged goodbye, both crying a little, not from loss but from the end of a now-comfortable norm on which the light was going out. Claire was dreading coming back to an empty house. And Mary knew it and felt for her.

"I'll call you on Sunday to make sure you get home okay," Mary said.

"I'd like that," responded Claire, kissing Ty on his cold cheek.

The three cars left at the same time, one going south and the other two going north.

***

As Mary in her car and Andy in the big SUV pulled up along the curb across the street from his parents' house, Mary noticed a Christmas tree through the picture window at the front of the house. She walked over and opened Holly's door in time to hear, "Oh for heaven's sake! Can't they wait one single day? It's like no one even celebrates Thanksgiving anymore. It's just a big meal lost somewhere in the ever-elongating lead-up to Christmas. I think it's sad."

"I don't know," replied Andy. "If Christmas is about Christ, what should we be more thankful for than Him and His birth? Besides, who doesn't love the look and smell of a Christmas tree any time of year?"

Holly screwed up her face and was just about to retort when Mary offered, "Holly, you all look so nice dressed up, you can take a picture in front of the tree and have your Christmas card picture ready the day after Thanksgiving." This brightened Holly's demeanor noticeably and she was friendly as they entered the houseful of confusion, movement, memory-filled smells, and talk.

Most of Andy's family had met Mary at some time in the past. They were friendly to her and Ty, trying to engage her in conversation and learning about her moving to North Pine. After the delicious meal (and because the weather was unusually warm with no snow on the ground), the great backyard football battle commenced. The game claimed only one moderately hyperextended knee, some sore shoulders, part of a pair of khakis, and some memories of athletic glory. When the game finally fell apart, Andy walked triumphantly back into the house. "To the victors go the spoils," he said as he headed for the pies, carelessly letting flap the torn back pocket to his pants that showed a bit of his underwear.

"Andy, you're showing the world your undies," scolded Holly.

Bill took some duct tape from a drawer next to the refrigerator, tore off a six-inch length and handed it to Andy, who taped up his pocket. "Problem solved," he said as he resumed serving up pies.

"I hope you've got a lot more of that tape, the way you're plowing through those pies," Holly said and then smiled as though she meant it as a joke. The room went still for a moment. Andy chewed the bite he had taken enough to say, "I do," and winked at her.

"While we're all sweaty," he announced, "Can you guys help me move Mary and Ty into Matt and Jimmy's old bedroom?"

The trailer was emptied within fifteen minutes. Mary's things that she didn't put in the furnished room were stored in the deep garage among boxes and half-made (or maybe half-fallen-apart) wood furniture. A few minutes later Ty was asleep on fresh sheets in the crib in their new room.

* * *

"You're still a guest here," Sharon said, but Mary wouldn't give up the dishcloth.

"No," she responded, "I'm part of the household now. I live here, and I'll help out all I want."

Holly rolled her eyes as she zipped up her kids' jackets, preparing to leave.

Sharon turned to Andy. "Are you sure you have to leave? We have plenty of room and clean linens. We'd love to have you guys stay an extra day."

"Mom, you've had plenty of commotion around here for one weekend." Bill grunted his agreement from in front of the TV. "We'll spend a night between Christmas and New Year's," Andy said, immediately realizing he hadn't discussed this idea with Holly and glancing guiltily in her direction. She wasn't looking at him, but the set of her jaw assured him they would discuss it on the ride home.

Mary saw it too. "I'll be so homesick by Christmas, you'll have to come and see me. I'll have my own place by then, but I'm sure Sharon and Bill won't mind me coming over," she said with a questioning inflection aimed at Sharon.

"Of course not. Heavens, if I have it my way you'll still be here at Christmas. There's nothing as sweet as a baby at Christmas. Isn't that what it's all about? A baby?" She chuckled daintily at her joke.

Holly seemed to relax at the thought that Mary would be there to soften the landing, and she gave Mary a tight hug as the little family left. "If you need anything, let me know. Andy has a lot of friends up here who can help you. And if you need to blow off some steam, give me a call," she said with a sideways glance at Sharon.

"I'll be fine," Mary replied.

Bill got out of his chair to hug the dearly departing. Andy's duct tape came lose and his pocket waved goodbye as he walked out to the street.

Chapter 6

Sharon insisted no paid baby sitter would rob her of the joy of taking care of Ty during Mary's first week at work. "Did you see those strapping boys I raised? I'll do a whole lot more than keep him alive. We'll have a great time together. Go on."

On her way to her first day at Black Star, Mary thought about the church service she had attended with Sharon and Bill the day before. Mary had always had a good relationship with her God. She talked to Him a lot and felt like He was watching out for her. Even in hard times like when Mark died, Mary believed that her Father loved her and she could see His work in little experiences that others might have ignored, like the fact that when she was pregnant and would visit Mark's grave, the baby would kick more vigorously than at any other time. She liked to think it was because their three spirits were talking in ways no body could sense or reason.

She remembered one incident about two weeks after Mark's funeral. She was looking at a photo album she had put together. One of the pictures was of Mary looking overly sad at a plate of slightly burned chocolate-chip cookies. She smiled and cried as she remembered how Mark would say, "You're treating me like the gods, giving me burnt offerings."

Later that night after crying at the photo, as she was dreading going to her lonely bed, there was a reluctant knock at the door. She looked at the clock, wondering who it could be so late. Looking through the peephole, she saw a woman slowly backing away from the door with a plate in her hands. Mary turned on the porch light and opened the door to her neighbor Amy.

"I'm sorry," said Amy, returning quickly to the door. Mary met her the first time when moving in. Amy was friendly, but too busy to be a hang-out-with friend. She attended Mark's funeral, and often gave very sincere-looking smiles as they passed each other on the stairs. She stood now in Mary's doorway in sweat pants and a baggy T-shirt. Mary had never seen her with glasses on until now.

"Sorry I'm dropping by so late," said Amy. "I just thought this afternoon that I should make you some cookies, but I put it off too long. And when I finally got around to it, I overcooked them a little. I was just going to throw them out and start fresh tomorrow, but I thought. . . . Oh, I don't know," she said as she handed over the plate.

"Chocolate-chip?" Mary asked.

"Am I that predictable?" Amy laughed.

"I love them already," Mary replied, choking a little on her words. "Thanks," she said quickly and started to close the door to preempt her breakdown.

Amy cocked her head to one side and looked concerned. "Mary?" she asked.

Mary broke. The tears came freely and Amy stepped into the apartment, closed the door and hugged her gently. "I'm so sorry," she said.

"Please, don't be," Mary responded. "These 'overcooked' cookies are an answer to prayers." She explained about the memory and the picture she had been looking at earlier that day. She also told Amy she was pregnant.

An hour later, after the second text message from her husband, Amy said as she left, "It's good to know it was God who burned my cookies and not me."

But those experiences came infrequently for Mary, and she felt lonely and sometimes abandoned. She continued to pray like she was talking to a friend and noticed the tiny miracles He gave her.

* * *

Mary hoped she would be early to her first day of work to start out with a good impression. But Betty the receptionist was already there, competent as ever. After having Mary fill out her

W-4 and other paperwork, she guided her to the QA department, a pair of medium-sized rooms and a small office with windows looking out onto the shop floor.

"Wait in this chair until Glen gets here," Betty commanded. She gave a small shrug for no apparent reason and left. Mary stood to get a better look at her surroundings. The chair was next to the door of the inner office. On the door were two small placards slid into holders. The top one said GLEN McCANN, and the one just below it said MANAGER, QUALITY ASSURANCE. She peered into the office, lit through the big window by the lights in the shop. It was oddly clean; no pictures on the wall, no knickknacks on the desk. There was a copy of the company's mission statement taped to the side of a filing cabinet, but otherwise the room was pretty bare.

"I heard we had a new girl coming in," came a cheery voice from behind her. Startled, Mary spun around to see a young 20-something like herself putting on a baggy, light-blue lab coat. "C'mon over and get suited up," said the girl. Another showed up. The first introduced herself as Lisa. "Put on a coat, some booties—oh girl, you're not going to want to wear heels here; they tear right through the booties—and grab a pair of high-fashion glasses," she smiled as she tossed Mary a pair of oversized protective goggles. "You'll need a hair net, too. Now you're looking as unattractive as possible," she said with a big grin. "Wait, you'll need some latex gloves—just in case you have nice hands, you can cover them. There," she said as Mary took the gloves, "Your ensemble is complete."

The second girl said somewhat under her breath and looking toward the door, "It's not unattractive enough for some people."

Just then Glen McCann shooed in two other girls. "Hope you all had a great Thanksgiving. Did you give thanks for this great job?" The girls all turned to their stations. Glen hurried over to Mary, "You must be Mary Comardy! Russ . . . Mr. Carter said you'd be joining us, but he didn't tell us how much you brighten up a room."

Mary shook his hand firmly, looking him in the eye. "I'm glad to be a part of the team. And I'm eager to learn. Do you want me to train with one of these ladies?"

"No, come on into my office. We'll have a sit-down-get-to-know-you session before we start with the workaday stuff. No, not there," he said as she walked toward the chair in front of his desk. "Have a seat on the couch. That way, there's no big desk acting as a psychological barrier between us, and we can really get to know each other."

Mary was glad for the oversized lab coat that she could wrap around her knees. Her knee-length skirt and the low couch weren't a modest combination. She regretted not asking about the dress code earlier, but she had thought she would just sit through some long orientation on her first day.

Glen leaned forward on the chair in front of her, "So, tell me about yourself. I didn't get to interview you, so I'd like to get to know who I'm working with here."

Although she hadn't practiced her "elevator pitch of me" since she landed the job, she managed to remember and recite it pretty well.

"You already got the job; this isn't an interview," Glen smiled. "I want to know the real you. Where'd you grow up? What's your family like? That kind of stuff."

"Well, I'm a widowed mother of a baby boy," she said twisting her wedding ring.

"I'm sorry to hear that."

"I'm from Sunset, down south about two hours. I was raised by a saint of a woman who taught me to work. I was about a year from going to college when my husband died. My little boy has changed my career plans, needless to say. I worked at Rockwell and became a cell captain there before they closed."

"Huh. All the other girls are single with no kids. So this job is pretty important to you, I guess. Otherwise you wouldn't have moved all the way from Sunset.

"I hope you don't decide to mother all of us," he said chuckling. "What's your favorite food?" he pivoted. "We go out to a quarterly lunch, and we might just let you choose where we go since you're the new girl."

"I'm pretty easy to please, I guess," Mary responded, wondering at the line of questioning. "I like Mexican food."

"Everybody likes Mexican food; what else have you got? What's your secret sinful indulgence? French bon-bons? Pig's feet?"

"I'm pretty average in my food tastes. Nothing unusual. My family couldn't afford anything exotic. I guess I'm a grilled chicken salad kind of girl," she said warily. Then trying to change the subject, she asked "How long have you been the QA manager?"

"Oh, I've been at Black Star for about eight years. I got promoted to QA manager 18 months ago. This is a great place to work, especially this department. We like to have fun. Out on the shop floor, you can't talk, but in here, there's not much noise, so there's a lot of socializing, and I let it happen. What are a bunch of women going to do sitting around in a room all day? They're going to talk, and they do, but I let them. I kind of like listening, getting a woman's perspective on things."

"I don't see any men in the department. Are there any?"

"You mean besides me?" Glen feigned offense. "No, I find that women are better suited to the work. Their hands are quicker and less clumsy than some ham-handed man. And they can focus better.

"Wait, are you from the EEOC?" he asked jokingly, then suddenly straight-faced he continued, "Not that we don't take that stuff seriously here. We don't want any trouble, but we like to observe the *spirit* of the law here.

"Do you breastfeed?" he asked almost suddenly.

"Wha...? Wh...?"

"We're a very mother-friendly company. We have a mother's lounge where you can pump if you want. Or even if you want someone to bring in your little boy, you can nurse him in there on break. It's been done before." He sat looking at her as if still expecting a reply to his question.

"I'll keep that in mind," she finally said.

He crossed his legs and interlaced his fingers around his knee. "So what did you do in high school? Cheerleader? Track? You don't seem very dramatic, so no drama?"

"Uh, I was mostly on the newspaper staff."

"A reporter! Exposés and investigative journalism, no doubt! Did you ever get anyone suspended? Or fired?"

"No, I worked on the Features section. Student spotlights, clubs, new staff, that sort of thing."

"Your own little *Seventeen* magazine, eh?"

There was a noise outside his office that momentarily attracted Glen's attention, and Mary took the opening.

"Well, I'm anxious to see what the work is and get started learning," she said moving to the edge of the couch, hoping this hint would lead him to begin some kind of training.

"Okay, well, I guess we've gotten to know each other okay—for the first day. Don't be a stranger, though. I have an open-door policy," he said gesturing toward the closed door. "If you have any questions, or just want to talk—it doesn't even have to be about work—just come on in."

He got up, and she sprang off the couch immediately to follow him to the door. He stopped abruptly and spun so that she, following too closely, collided with him.

"Oh, my," he said with a wide smile. "Excuse me." Then he turned, opened the door, and summoned Lisa. "I think you two met earlier? Lisa, can you train Mary on Station Two?"

As Mary left the room, Glen put his hand in the small of her back to send her out of the room, and kept contact with her just a half-second too long.

Lisa signaled her to sit at a chair in front of a pair of small identical machines. On the left side of the machines was a light blue bin. On the right side of the machines were two dark blue bins of the same size. Lisa counted out four very small metal objects from the light blue bin. "These are fuel injector nozzles for car engines," she said. "You take four of them and slip two into the two slots in this machine and two in the other. Then you close the glass and simply push this green button. The lasers measure the nozzle opening. If it's okay, the green button flashes three times. Then you take the good nozzles out and put them in the indigo bin. If one of these red lights goes on, there's a problem with the nozzle above it. If that happens, you take that nozzle and another out, trade their places, and retest them. There's a legend that there was once a false rejection, but I've never seen one. They make us retest anyway.

"If the retest confirms the rejection, then you pick up this phone and tell the voice on the other end that you've got a rejection for this lot number, the one on the card on the side of the blue bin."

"Which blue bin?"

"This is blue; that's indigo. The bins follow the colors of the rainbow as they progress through the line. Remember Roy G. Biv. Red, orange, yellow, green, blue, indigo, violet. Roy G. Biv. Indigo means they've been QA certified and are ready for packaging and shipping. If you have no rejects in a bin, you initial the QA box on the card and transfer the card to the indigo bin. Easy enough?"

"Sure."

"How was your first meeting with Glen?"

Mary looked up into Lisa's eyes, trying to divine how loaded the question was.

"He's different," she said.

"Did he come onto you?" Lisa asked quietly.

Mary was shocked at the blunt question. The woman at Station Three heard the question, and turned to hear the answer.

"Uh, not exactly," she said, still wary.

"McHands is pretty harmless."

"McHands?"

"Yeah. McCann? McHands? He flirts, but he never tries to close the deal. He's either a chicken or he's the slyest sexual harasser there ever was. Everything he does can be interpreted as innocent, but some of us feel different. The problem is that he's Mr. Carter's nephew, so that and his carefulness make it so no one wants to report him. Besides, I think he likes having us all off balance. If he ever made a real move, we'd all know he's just a creep. But where there's nothing for sure, he gets some sick power trip from it.

"Girls who can't take it quit. Those of us who stick around, well, you just get used to it and ignore it. It's really not that bad."

Mary glanced over at McHands's office. He was standing in the doorway, leaning against the side post and looking at her with a broad smile on his face.

Chapter 7

As she pushed Ty's stroller between the racks of discounted clothes, Mary was startled to hear her name from a man. McHands? She turned around to see a familiar face that took her a second to put a name to. "Simon?" she said shaking her head to clear the cobwebs. She smiled, happy to see someone who looked a little like Mark.

"I thought that was you," he said. "Didn't expect to see you here in the Small." This was what the locals called their tiny mall. "I haven't seen you since Mark's funeral."

"I took a job here and moved up with little Ty." As soon as she said it, she remembered that she hadn't told Mark's family about his baby. She could see the concentrated look on Simon's face, and assumed he was doing the math on Ty's conception. She decided to spare him the effort. "I don't think you've met Tyson Mark Comardy." She picked up the baby. "This is your uncle Simon," she said to Ty in a sing-song voice.

Simon reached his hand out and wiggled the baby's wrist. "Hey, widdle fella," he said, then stopped briefly as he noticed his grandmother's ring on Mary's finger. "So, how're things going here in North Pine?"

"I'm staying temporarily with my sister's in-laws while I look for an apartment. I've got a job, and I'm starting to like it here."

"Well, I'm happy for you. You deserve it."

"Thanks, Simon."

An awkward silence set in, so they both said a tumbling goodbye with a friendly smile and went to browse elsewhere.

* * *

McCann was waiting near her car in the mall parking lot as she approached.

"I thought this was your car! And look at your little boy. Isn't he a handsome little man."

"Hi Glen."

"I guess in a small town like North Pine you run into people you know all the time," Glen said. "Hey, it looks like you're leaving, but would you want to go grab a bite to eat? Nothing fancy, just a sandwich or something. I'm buying."

"Sorry, Glen. I need to get Ty home."

"Do you have a baby-sitter for him?" McHands asked. "Oh, not for right now, but for another time when there's time to plan something."

"Are you asking me out?" Mary asked flatly.

"Of course not," he replied, taking a half step back. "I wouldn't want to jeopardize our budding working relationship," he smiled. "I just hoped that as friends we could hang out some evening, outside of the work environment where we can leave work behind and really get to know each other."

Mary's mind raced. If she said no, would she put her job in danger? She didn't want to say yes, simply because she didn't like him. She prided herself on being able to read people pretty well, but she couldn't get a bead on McHands. His motives seemed so opaque.

"Another time, maybe," she said, grateful that Ty began to fuss.

"Okay," McHands said cheerfully, holding the door and watching as she put Ty into his seat. "We'll talk about it another time. See you Monday," he called over his shoulder as he walked toward the mall.

Chapter 8

Mary's cell phone vibrated late, just as she was drifting off. It startled her awake, shocking her body into delayed reaction. She quickly reached for the phone, trying to stop the buzzing before it woke up Ty, Sharon or Bill.

"Hello?" she whispered hoarsely.

"Mary? This is Simon." Mary's mind was still clouded. "Mark's brother, Simon."

"Oh. Hi Simon," she whispered, glancing at the baby boy stirring in his crib. He was waking. She knew the only chance to keep him asleep was to rock him, so she took him from the crib and cradled him in her arms and swayed, trying at the same time to pinch the small cell phone between her shoulder and ear. Then, to prevent waking Sharon and Bill in the next room, Mary tiptoed quickly down the hall to another used-to-be bedroom.

Sharon called this the "sewing room," but it looked like it had been a while since any sewing was done here. Fabric scraps were piled high around the sewing machine on a small old kitchen table. A cedar chest sat under the window, piled high with pillows and a chair turned upside down. There were stacks of faded construction paper and other craft supplies on a rickety shelf, and a closet filled with empty boxes marked "Christmas decor". In the corner, with a flag rolled loosely behind it, sat a rocking chair occupied by a box. Mary stood and swayed.

As she had moved from one room to the next, Simon apologized. "Sorry for calling so late. I debated whether to call you at all, and ultimately decided I needed to. I think I made a big mistake. Well, I know I did, but I didn't mean to."

Mary waited.

"I was at a family Christmas party last night and mentioned having seen you. And I mentioned your little Ty."

Mary stopped swaying, then started again as Ty began to grimace in the dim light provided where faint light shone through the window.

"My mom started to cry, and that made my two sisters pretty upset. You didn't get to know them well—Mark probably shielded you from them—but they kind of feed off each other. By the end of the evening, they were talking about suing you for visitation rights for my parents to see your baby."

It seemed the air refused to enter Mary's lungs. She bent over a little, hunched over Ty, still pinching the phone into her neck.

"You still there?" Simon asked.

"Yeah," she whispered.

"I'm really sorry. I didn't mean for it to go like this. I thought they'd be happy for you and happy that Mark had a baby. I really didn't consider it might go sideways like that."

"Yeah," she breathed, barely audible.

"I feel totally responsible. I told them it was crazy to make a big deal about it, but they don't listen to me. Look, if they really do start into something like this, I'll be on your side. Mark loved you so much. I know you're a great mom. And I realize you did what you had to when he was in the hospital."

"Yeah," she wept.

"I didn't want to wake you up, but I knew I couldn't live with myself if you heard about this before I could tell you. Is there anything I can do to help right now?"

"No," she wept again.

"I should have waited until morning. I'm really sorry about this, calling late, and the bad news. All of it." He waited, hoping she would say something, but knowing she couldn't.

"Okay, well, let me know if I can do anything for you. I'm really sorry. I'll try to call you tomorrow."

"Okay, bye," she whispered, trembling, tears finding their way down to her chin. The phone clicked off. Because she couldn't take it from her ear, she leaned over and let it fall to the carpet. A tear fell onto Ty's neck, and he shivered. She realized for the first time how cold it was in this room. There was a baby quilt hanging on the wall, beautiful in its homemade simplicity, causing Mary to pause as she reached for it. She remembered a story by Alice Walker about another hand-made quilt and took it from the rod, draping it over her shoulder and Ty. He shuddered a little at the cold quilt, and even whimpered, but it caught and held his and her body heat quickly, and he relaxed.

"Dear Father!" she screamed in her mind. "Haven't I suffered enough?" She leaned her head back, trying to look through the ceiling and the roof to see if anyone was listening, and realized that her neck was sore from holding the phone so uncomfortably. She laughed cynically to herself. "There's your answer," she thought.

Her head hung. She cried onto the quilt. Slowly, the quilt seemed to begin to glow. She realized it was the moon escaping the clouds and streaming through a gap between the two curtain panels. The beam illuminated a particular block of fabric with a faded illustration of a small girl praying in her bed and a guardian angel kneeling at the bedside. Ty nuzzled her arm, giggled, and released a big sigh, settling into the cradle of her arms. She looked at the fabric block again, and the thought entered her head, "You know he's there." She felt a soft warmth that came from within her, too consistent to be a result of the quilt.

"Okay," she whispered, "It's in Your hands." She stayed in the cool room, enjoying the warm feeling within and swaying Ty, until she heard Bill begin snoring from his bedroom. Mary tiptoed back to her room, put a heavy Ty back into his crib, and lay in bed feeling alternately dread and gratitude.

Only a few hours later, Ty started coughing.

Chapter 9

By seven o'clock that morning, Ty's breathing was noticeably quicker and he was congested. Mary thought about leaving him with Sharon, but decided to call in sick.

"I hope your boy gets better soon. We really miss you here already," Glen said over the phone.

The rapid breathing and wet cough concerned Mary, but the look on Sharon's face convinced her. Mary loaded Ty into his car seat and headed for the pediatrician's office, who ricocheted her to the local emergency room.

"Normally in older children, RSV manifests just as a minor cold," the Emergency Department physician said in a well-practiced script. "But for infants and young toddlers it can have complications. We'll keep," she glanced at the chart, "Ty here for a few hours to observe him. We've started a breathing treatment, and we'll try to keep his passages clear of heavy mucus. He may have to stay overnight."

Mary's eyebrows scrunched together.

"That's only if he doesn't respond to the breathing treatment, which isn't common. And if it *is* necessary, it will only be a precaution. Occasionally, things turn south and we have to keep kids for a couple of days for more intensive interventions. And in very rare cases, it can get serious. But let's not wander any farther down that path than we have to at this point," she said with a reassuring smile while reaching out to touch Mary's arm.

The doctor continued, "Ty seems comfortable right now, so we'll let him rest and let the breathing treatment do its job. The nurses will check on him every half-hour, and I'll be back later to check on both of you. Let us know if you need anything."

As she left, another person entered who had been at the reception desk when Mary first entered the ER. Ty had been admitted immediately because there was no one else in the waiting room. "Thank goodness for small-town ERs," thought Mary. They got Ty quickly back to a room and the doctor had arrived within just a few minutes.

The lady from the reception desk said, "Hi, I'm Tammy, and I need to collect the rest of your payment information," and swung the wall-mounted keyboard and monitor up to her waist. She confirmed personal details, and then asked for insurance.

"My son is on the state insurance program," Mary said. She thought she saw a flash of disapproval on Tammy's face, but if it happened, it was gone in a moment. Mary forced the thought into her mind that it was okay, but she didn't believe herself. She hated being dependent on anyone. She was taught that if she wanted something, she earned it. But Ty shouldn't have to suffer because his mom got laid off. She set her jaw and finished the process, producing the Medicaid cards and supplying the requested information.

Tammy left, and Mary curled up in her chair. It was only mid-afternoon, but she felt exhausted. Then she remembered the call with Simon the night before. Sitting in the hospital, next to her struggling son, missing work with a boss she couldn't anticipate a reaction from, and trying not to think of the worst possible scenario of what might happen with Mark's family finally overcame her. She began to cry, a silent but open and clean cry, her tears running freely onto the tan fake-leather upholstery of the chair.

Ty was officially admitted and transferred to a regular room late that evening and held overnight "for more observation; just to be safe." Mary lay in the fold-down chair in the room. Through the night she would almost get into a deep sleep just as the nurse would come by for the hourly visit. Thankfully she slept through the fifth visit, but couldn't sleep thereafter.

By mid-morning of the next day, Ty's condition had not improved like it was supposed to. His chest was still sucking in way too far ("sternal retractions" they called it) with each breath, showing that he was laboring hard for his air. Mary stood by, helpless and anxious as the kind nurses narrated and explained their actions to soothe her.

Sharon and Bill came at noon, and Sharon coaxed Mary out of the room for a quick lunch while Bill stayed.

"Dear girl, that boy is strong," Sharon said sitting next to Mary in the hospital cafeteria. "He's going to be okay. Give him a little more time to win." She said all the right things to give Mary hope, but just as she started to feel optimistic, the memory of Simon's phone call crashed into her mind. She told Sharon about it, and again Sharon knew what to say. They sat together for a moment, Mary's hands together on the table, Sharon's hand on top of them, Mary's forehead on top of Sharon's hand, and Sharon's other hand rubbing the back of Mary's neck and the base of her skull.

As they returned to the room, Sharon said, "If they haven't released him by seven o'clock tonight, I'm going to come back and you're going to go home with Bill."

"I'm not...."

"Don't argue with me, young lady. You're going to go home and get some rest. You can come back tomorrow morning. I'll call you if anything happens."

"What if...."

"I'll call you if anything happens," Sharon said more slowly and emphatically.

They left Mary alone again with her son. She called her mom for a satisfying cry, and her sister for a less-satisfying lecture about how she shouldn't trust the doctors to know what's best. She thought about calling work again; she had called in that morning and intentionally left a message for Glen with Betty because she didn't want to talk to him. She knew her job was in jeopardy, but she felt too emotionally wobbly to discuss it.

Shortly after seven o'clock when the doctors made the decision to keep Ty overnight again, Sharon and Bill arrived. Sharon had things to keep her busy through the coming sleeplessness, and gave Mary a kiss on the forehead as Bill ushered Mary out of the room.

Mary slept in the car the fifteen minutes to the Taylor's house.

Chapter 10

Mary opened the door to the sewing room and walked to the quilt hung on the wall. She touched it softly, then rubbed it, then grabbed it tightly. She felt nothing.

"Please, God," she whispered, "I need this right now."

She moved the box from the seat of the old rocking chair and sat heavily onto the dust-free square left by the box. She wept. Her head bowed, and her hands came up to support it. Her weeping became more intense, and she felt her trembling hands couldn't support her head anymore, so she lay it back, her hands hanging over the arm rests.

"Why is this happening to me?" she sobbed. "God, why can't this pain be spread around a little? There are plenty of people who seem perfectly happy, who could take a little of this. Why me and not them?"

She thought she heard a very soft knock at the door. Not sure if it was at her door or another, she softly answered, "Yes?"

Bill opened the door gently as Mary wiped away tears.

"Is everything okay?" he asked. As she began to respond, he cut her off. "Let me rephrase that; I think you need some company right now," he said walking into the room. He pulled the upside down chair off the cedar chest, set it upright a few feet in front of her, and stood behind it for a moment. "You must be asking yourself some pretty heavy questions right now."

"Not myself," she responded. "God."

"So?"

She looked away.

"I've been there." He paused for a few seconds, then walked around the chair and sat in it, leaning forward. "Mind if I give it a whack?"

"Give what a whack?"

"Trying to answer your questions."

A painful but grateful breath jumped from her lungs that sounded like a doubtful laugh. Bill didn't acknowledge it.

"Why you?" Bill tested.

"That's a good start."

"Let's start further back. Why are you here?"

"At your house, or on this miserable planet?"

"On this sometimes miserable, sometimes magical planet."

Mary softened a bit, thinking of the magic Ty brought into her life. "I always thought it was to learn to love. But it seems everything I love gets taken from me. Mark; education;

good jobs; my mom lives hours away; and now my boy's health, my sense of security for our little family?" She started to weep again.

Bill handed her a handkerchief, which she gratefully accepted.

"You're right," he said. "And you've learned a lot of loving. That's why it hurts so much."

"Did He put us here to hurt? I've always thought he loved us, but now it seems kind of cruel to put us here only to be disappointed in the end."

"You can only feel disappointment, sorrow, and pain if you love. If you didn't love and care, you wouldn't feel disappointment. You'd be numb, concrete. The fact that we feel pain and sorrow means that we've felt love."

Mary sighed. "I'll give you all that. Sometimes accidents happen, or we bring pain on ourselves. But why doesn't He stop terrible people from doing terrible things? Or stop terrible things from happening to innocent people, like babies? Does it have to be as bad as it is? Couldn't He make it a little . . . easier?"

"No."

"Huh? What kind of God can't tweak things a little to make life easier here?"

"Sometimes He does, but mostly He doesn't, because, first, he's never going to take away our right to choose, even to choose evil; and, second, well, that brings us to the answer to the original question of why we are here. To learn to love is only part of the answer. The whole answer is 'to learn to love as He loves.'

Bill continued, "Can you imagine the disappointment He feels watching the way His children treat each other? We do terrible things to each other, and He still loves us. Why doesn't he stop it? Well, how could we learn if the Teacher were constantly making the content easier? How far would we get? If we're going to somehow, someday, some way, be perfect even as He is perfect, He can't dumb down the lessons and the tests. We're here to learn and to take tests."

"I'm failing the tests."

"Oh darlin', you're acing them. Your kindness endures. Your love endures. The fact that you're asking these questions means you want to learn. You're on the right path, but it's a hard one. Jesus, Robert Frost and Stephen Crane all said so. The difficult path is one of the most frequently recurring topics in all of human history. But what would you trade it for? Easier paths are out there, lots of them, but they lead to places of stunted love, reduced joy, and fleeting pleasures that leave holes in the soul."

"I have some pretty big holes in my own soul right now," Mary said with pain just shy of anger. "So why work so hard when you end up in the same situation?"

"Your holes are in your heart, not your soul."

Mary looked a little frustrated.

"Sorry, but it's true," he protested, smiling a little. "Holes in the heart happen when life hurts us. Holes in the soul happen when we walk away from God's path."

Mary's frustration turned to confusion.

"Look at Jesus," Bill said. "He wept. He wept a lot. His suffering was beyond our understanding at the end, but He kept His soul whole by following the path His Father assigned Him.

"But even He had to learn how. He wasn't brought to the world as King Jesus, or General Jesus. He was born Baby Jesus, in a stable in a small village to a tradesman and his wife. In the Bible it says He grew in wisdom. This means He learned. And my guess is that He learned in pretty much the same way we do. Maybe He learned better, made better choices, and probably had some angelic tutors, but He had to learn the same things we do.

"And here's the great part: because of this, He knows how we feel. Lots of people say, 'I know how you feel,' but He really does.

"Y'know, there's a last verse to the carol 'It Came upon the Midnight Clear' that doesn't get sung a lot. It goes like this, if I can remember it right." He looked up as though the lyrics were written on his forehead and hummed briefly, then sang.

"And ye, beneath life's crushing load,

Whose forms are bending low,

Who toil along the climbing way

With painful steps and slow,

Look now! for glad and golden hours

come swiftly on the wing.

O rest beside the weary road,

And hear the angels sing!"

"That's actually really nice," she said. "But I don't hear any angels singing, just you talking."

Bill laughed. "My singing certainly isn't angelic, I know. But here's the thing: all those people who sat along the weary road to hear the angels sing—they all eventually had to stand up, pick up their loads, and keep climbing. They may have felt their loads lighter, but they still had to carry them. I'm sorry that this season, that should be so fun, has been so hard for you this year. But you're doing just what you should. And you'll have your time to celebrate."

Mary looked away.

"I know you've seen miracles. We all have."

"Not me," she responded, shaking her head.

"Are you sure? They're usually pretty small. Things like, after saying a little prayer, finding your glasses or keys in the same place you've looked twice already. I think God gives us little miracles to let us know He's there when we want big miracles but He knows better than to give them to us. Some people want to call the little miracles coincidences. I choose to believe they're miracles, and I've seen hundreds of them."

Mary thought again about the burnt cookies and making it close enough to the gas station to give a couple of nice teenagers the opportunity to help her.

"Look," Bill said. "I don't think Jesus was really born in late December, but I like that we have Christmas just before the end of the year, because it's a new beginning. Everything changed that day. Everything got better. It didn't get easier, but it got better. And just because you can't see them doesn't mean angels aren't surrounding you right now on a special mission from

God to help His faithful daughter through this time. I truly believe that. You're worth it to Him."

Mary sighed with gratitude and exhaustion. Bill's words had struck deep within her with a meaning and gravity that she had felt only a few other times in her life. "Why do you pretend to be such a curmudgeon?" she asked him smiling a little.

"I don't know what you're talking about," he said. His voice had changed back to that of the old man who sat in front of the TV, but there was a twinkle in his eye.

"We better get you to bed," he said. As she stood up, the corner of the quilt hanging on the wall began to flutter just a little. Mary saw it, and so did Bill.

"Dangit," he said. "I really wish that woman would close the heat vent when she's done in this room." He walked over to the register to close it. "There's no one in here for weeks at a time. No sense heating the place when no one's in here, right?"

She agreed, and watched the quilt settle. She smiled.

Chapter 11

Ty's condition turned that night. By the time Mary got to the hospital in the morning, he was alert. When she walked in the room he gave her a big smile, a lively squeal, and an enthusiastic flailing of his arms and legs. Once in the car, she reached back uncomfortably and held his tiny hand until the feeling had gone from her arm.

After returning to the Taylors' in the late clear and cold morning on December 22, Mary called Glen.

"I'll be coming to work tomorrow," she said. She had predetermined not to ask *if* she could go to work, in case that made any difference.

"Don't bother," Glen said.

"Wh…. You're…. Are you firing me?"

"Oh, heavens no," laughed Glen a little too energetically. "I just mean you don't have to come in. You'll still have your job next week after Christmas."

"But I can't afford to miss any more days."

"Don't worry. It's taken care of," Glen replied. "You stay home with that baby boy."

"What do you mean, 'It's taken care of'? I really can't afford it. I need the money."

"I really have to go to a meeting. Can you talk in an hour? Merry Christmas!" Glen said, ending the call before she could answer.

"I better take care of this," she said to Sharon, who had been listening to the one side of the conversation. "Can you watch Ty again while I run down to the work?"

"You go take care of that. I'll snuggle this little snowflake until he melts," she said squeezing Ty gently and dramatically.

***

As Mary walked into the front office, Betty said flatly, "I thought you weren't coming back until after Christmas."

"I just had a weird conversation on the phone with Glen, and I need to talk to him."

"Glen should be just finishing up with Mr. Carter," replied Betty. "I guess you can wait here for him to come out of the office."

Mary sat in the same spot she had taken weeks before, feeling the same anxiety she had felt then. What if she lost her job? How long would the Taylors put up with her? Would she have to move back to Sunset?

Glen came out of the office and looked authentically surprised when Mary stood and walked toward him.

"Glen, I don't think I got a full understanding of what you were saying on the phone," Mary began, quoting the lines she had rehearsed in her mind.

"Oh, okay. Um, let's talk about it then." He turned to Betty. "Is the interview room occupied?" he asked her.

"On the twenty-second of December?" she retorted.

"Come this way," he said. She could tell he was off kilter. Maybe he'd just been yelled at by Mr. Carter.

"Right in here," he said, opening a door with a small window into a small room with a small card table and two folding chairs.

Mary chose the chair facing the door, as if it were her office, feeling that it gave her a position of power. She sat with her feet flat on the floor and her hands flat on the table.

"Please explain to me," she demanded calmly, "what you meant by what you said on the phone."

"Well, I said there's nothing for you to worry about," he said with a sudden smile.

"No, you actually said, 'Don't worry about it.'"

His smile disappeared. He looked a little hurt. "I'm really sorry. I didn't mean to fluster you. You should be home taking care of your boy."

"Just explain what you do mean," she demanded again.

He paused. "Um, I'd rather not."

Mary's eyes flashed, and she could see he was digging in, but he had the look of a boy facing the willow switch for a friend. She stepped back mentally. "I want to keep this job," she said. "Is it possible, or is it already over? I know I didn't have any time off to cover my absence. Tell me straight; is my time at Black Star over?"

"Oh, it's not over," he said, daring to smile again. Mary exhaled sharply to show her exasperation. He continued, "The girls in the department asked if they could pitch in hours they had saved up for Christmas, just one or two hours each. I thought it was a great idea and took it to HR, telling them about your little boy, and about your husband dying, too."

Mary felt somewhat violated at this, but Glen kept going so quickly that she couldn't interrupt.

"HR got on board and asked if anyone else wanted to contribute an hour or two. What I'm saying is that you're covered, even through New Year's, if you want to be." Mary's mouth opened slightly and involuntarily. Glen resumed, "In fact, one person contributed two whole days! HR is sworn to secrecy. Nobody knows who it is except the person and the HR director."

Mary felt lighter. Her shoulders relaxed and her head raised. "Glen," she said after a pause that caused Glen to squirm a little, "I don't know what to say. That was a very kind thing for you and the girls to do." She paused, and then plunged. "I have to admit that I didn't expect something like that from you. Glen, why can't I get a read on you? I'm usually a pretty good judge of character, but I can't figure you out. What am I missing?"

"Oh, that," Glen responded less enthusiastically.

"I didn't mean to offend or hurt you," Mary said quickly. "You don't have to answer."

"It's okay. I think I know what you mean. I've been told I'm a little different. And I've been told that it's because I was raised by a mom with increasingly severe mental health problems. By the time I was seven, my dad had left, and that made things worse for her. She depended on me a lot, and so did my little brother, who has autism, but is pretty high functioning. I've known for a long time that I didn't live in a household of socially adept people, but I didn't know it had rubbed off on me so much until high school when a counselor finally pulled me aside and tried to talk to me about what's socially okay and what's not. See, I was always at home with two people who didn't behave normally, and so I really didn't learn to either. Ever since that talk with the counselor, I've just tried to be very friendly. I think I know what that looks like, so I try to do it."

He seemed pleased with himself, but an insecurity lingered behind his smile.

"Well, you certainly are friendly," Mary said, mostly to reassure him, and not sure if she really wanted to trust him. Was he just trying to gain her confidence to set her up for something? She decided she would give him the benefit of the doubt. "Thanks for helping me out with the time off. I really, really appreciate it. I'll be back to work after Christmas going full speed, I promise."

They left the interview room. Glen turned toward the QA department, and Mary turned toward the exit. "Merry Christmas," she said to Betty as she passed her desk. Betty gave her a close-lipped smile and said, "And to you," as she turned away. When Mary opened the door, a strong breeze blew in and pushed a sheet of paper off Betty's desk. She reached down, picked up the pay stub, and smiled to herself again looking at where it recorded a deduction of sixteen hours from her time-off balance.

As Mary reached for the car door handle, her phone's text tone rang. She climbed into the car, started it, and peeked at her phone, reading, "This is Simon. I talked to a lawyer friend. You have nothing to be concerned about. Sorry for worrying you.

Merry Christmas!"

Chapter 12

Christmas morning dawned bright white. Snow had fallen in large flakes through the night, covering the visible world with a pure white blanket, but the clouds were blowing away. Mary looked out at the bump on the side of the end of the Taylors' driveway. The day before, it was an ugly, jagged, graying, miniature alienscape, a remnant of a pile of snow and dirt that plows and shovels had heaped up. Now it was a perfectly smooth, gentle mound. She remembered Bill's words from a few days before, "Everything got better that day." Not that there wasn't still dirt under the blanket, but nature would eventually take care of that, too. Now was the time to 'rest beside the weary world and hear the angels sing.'

There were only a few gifts under the tree the Taylors shared with Mary and Ty, mostly for their grandchildren, some of whom would begin arriving around noon. The radio crooned a scratchy Christmas song that sounded black and white. The sharp but now-faint fir smell mixed with almond and maple aromas from Sharon's oven. Ty lay on his tummy near the tree alternating between drooling on a toy the Taylors had given him and stretching fruitlessly for the just-out-of-reach gifts.

Sharon returned from the kitchen where she had been checking on the magical contents of the oven, and sat down where she would have a good view of Ty. Bill was still seated in his chair, already fifteen pages into the Louis L'Amour book Sharon had given him.

"And here's something from me to the two of you," Mary said, retrieving a wrapped box that had seemed hidden beneath the tree. It was biggish, about fourteen inches square, but flatter, only three or four inches high.

"You shouldn't have," said Sharon, almost unsure she should receive it. "You need that money more than anything an old couple like us needs." But thinking that might sound ungrateful, she took the gift from Mary.

Mary realized it might look like a puzzle box and quickly instructed, "Don't shake it." Sharon unwrapped the plain cardboard box, looked at Mary, and cut open the tape with a pair of scissors. Inside lay a clock, somewhat plane in a classic way. But on the face were vinyl letters that had been carefully applied: *Watch of Wondering Love.*

"Watch of wondering love?" questioned Sharon.

"You know, from the song. 'While mortals sleep, the angels keep their watch of wondering love.' You two are my angels." Her voice started to falter. "You two have kept angelic watch over me and Ty for four of the hardest weeks of my life." She looked at Bill. "Some angels you can't see, but some are right in front of us.

"I wanted to buy you a set of matching watches and have them engraved, but I couldn't afford it." She continued before they could start their protests, "But I kind of hope this clock will always remind you of Ty and me and the power that kindness can have in people's lives."

"We'll be proud to hang this 'watch' in our house," Sharon said as she set it aside to give Mary a hug. When Sharon let go, Mary turned to Bill.

"C'mon Pops. I always wanted a 'Pops,'" she said as she half-dragged Bill to his feet where he gave her a warm and encompassing hug.

"You're a good kid," he said.

Mary returned to where she had been sitting. "I figure I'll finally be able to find a good place and move out by the end of January." Seeing Sharon's face fall a little, Mary quickly added, "We will come over a lot to visit, though—at least until you go on that church mission you talked about." Bill's eyebrows arched. Mary continued, "You said that it didn't feel like the right time before. I don't want to put words in God's mouth, but maybe your feelings were His way of telling you to hang around, because He knew I'd need you."

Bill smiled. "Well, it's something to think about," he said as a grandchild knocked on the front door and called, "Ho, Ho, Ho! Merry Christmas!"

ABOUT THE AUTHOR

DL Wilson loves Christmas year round and lives in Utah

with his wife and four children.

www.ingramcontent.com/pod-product-compliance
Lightning Source LLC
Chambersburg PA
CBHW020623130626
46552CB00003B/1081